Sweet Revenge

Eric and Wesley were standing right below the window. Jessica glanced at her sister and nodded. "Now," she whispered.

Elizabeth jumped up. She had a water balloon in each hand. She dropped them out the window. One balloon landed right on Eric's head. The other exploded on the grass and got both boys wet.

"Hey!" Eric and Wesley yelled. "Cut it out!"

"We got them!" Elizabeth yelled.

Jessica burst out laughing. She and Elizabeth had gotten back at the boys fair and square!

Bantam Skylark Books in the
SWEET VALLEY KIDS series

#1 SURPRISE! SURPRISE!
#2 RUNAWAY HAMSTER
#3 THE TWINS' MYSTERY TEACHER
#4 ELIZABETH'S VALENTINE
#5 JESSICA'S CAT TRICK
#6 LILA'S SECRET
#7 JESSICA'S BIG MISTAKE
#8 JESSICA'S ZOO ADVENTURE
#9 ELIZABETH'S SUPER-SELLING LEMONADE
#10 THE TWINS AND THE WILD WEST
#11 CRYBABY LOIS
#12 SWEET VALLEY TRICK OR TREAT
#13 STARRING WINSTON EGBERT
#14 JESSICA THE BABY-SITTER
#15 FEARLESS ELIZABETH
#16 JESSICA THE TV STAR
#17 CAROLINE'S MYSTERY DOLLS
#18 BOSSY STEVEN
#19 JESSICA AND THE JUMBO FISH
#20 THE TWINS GO TO THE HOSPITAL
#21 JESSICA AND THE SPELLING-BEE SURPRISE
#22 SWEET VALLEY SLUMBER PARTY
#23 LILA'S HAUNTED HOUSE PARTY
#24 COUSIN KELLY'S FAMILY SECRET
#25 LEFT-OUT ELIZABETH
#26 JESSICA'S SNOBBY CLUB
#27 THE SWEET VALLEY CLEANUP TEAM
#28 ELIZABETH MEETS HER HERO
#29 ANDY AND THE ALIEN
#30 JESSICA'S UNBURIED TREASURE
#31 ELIZABETH AND JESSICA RUN AWAY

SWEET VALLEY KIDS SUPER SNOOPER EDITIONS
#1 THE CASE OF THE SECRET SANTA
#2 THE CASE OF THE MAGIC CHRISTMAS BELL
#3 THE CASE OF THE HAUNTED CAMP

SWEET VALLEY KIDS

ELIZABETH AND JESSICA RUN AWAY

Written by
Molly Mia Stewart

Created by
FRANCINE PASCAL

Illustrated by
Ying-Hwa Hu

A BANTAM SKYLARK BOOK®
NEW YORK · TORONTO · LONDON · SYDNEY · AUCKLAND

To Lloyd D. Ribner III

RL 2, 005–008

ELIZABETH AND JESSICA RUN AWAY
A Bantam Skylark Book / August 1992

*Sweet Valley High® and Sweet Valley Kids are
trademarks of Francine Pascal*

Conceived by Francine Pascal

*Produced by Daniel Weiss Associates, Inc.
33 West 17th Street
New York, NY 10011*

Cover art by Susan Tang

*Skylark Books is a registered trademark of Bantam Books, a
division of Bantam Doubleday Dell Publishing Group, Inc.
Registered in U.S. Patent and Trademark Office and elsewhere.*

ISBN 0-553-48004-9

Published simultaneously in the United States and Canada

*Bantam Books are published by Bantam Books, a division of Ban-
tam Doubleday Dell Publishing Group, Inc. Its trademark,
consisting of the words "Bantam Books" and the portrayal of a
rooster, is Registered in U.S. Patent and Trademark Office and in
other countries. Marca Registrada. Bantam Books, 666 Fifth Ave-
nue, New York, New York 10103.*

PRINTED IN THE UNITED STATES OF AMERICA

OPM   0 9 8 7 6 5 4 3 2 1

CHAPTER 1

Out-of-Town Guests

"Do you know what today is?" Jessica Wakefield asked as she sat down at the breakfast table.

"Friday?" Mr. Wakefield guessed.

"Right," Jessica said. "That means today's the day we're being invaded by boys."

Jessica's twin sister, Elizabeth, looked up from her cinnamon toast. "When Eric and Wesley get here, we're going to swim and go to the park and ride bikes, and play kick-the-can and freeze tag," she said, sounding excited.

Eric Nelson was in the second grade, just

like Jessica and Elizabeth. His brother Wesley was one year younger. They were coming with their parents all the way from Oregon. Mr. Nelson had gone to law school with Mr. Wakefield. Eric and Wesley were going to stay with the Wakefields for the weekend while Mr. and Mrs. Nelson attended a business meeting in Los Angeles.

"You mean, *you're* going to swim and ride bikes and do that other stuff," Jessica corrected her sister. "*I* don't play with boys."

Elizabeth liked playing with boys. Jessica didn't. That was just one of the differences between them. Jessica and Elizabeth were identical twins. But just because they looked the same on the outside didn't mean that the twins were the same on the inside. Elizabeth enjoyed making up adventure stories and acting them out in the backyard, and she

played for the Sweet Valley Soccer League. Jessica didn't like soccer. She preferred less messy games such as hopscotch or jump rope. Jessica liked to wear pretty clothes, and she didn't like to get them dirty.

Despite their differences, even the twins' best friends sometimes had trouble telling them apart. Elizabeth and Jessica both had blue-green eyes and long, blond hair with bangs. When they wore matching outfits, it was almost impossible to tell which twin was which without looking at the name bracelets they always wore.

Being twins was special. Jessica and Elizabeth shared a bedroom, and they sat next to each other in school. Even though they liked different things, they knew they would always be best friends.

Mrs. Wakefield poured Jessica a glass of

orange juice. "Jessica, I hope you'll play with the boys at least a little. After all, Eric and Wesley have never been to Sweet Valley before. They're going to need lots of expert advice from all of us."

Jessica frowned. "What kind of expert advice?"

"They'll need someone to show them the way to the park," Mr. Wakefield said.

Mrs. Wakefield nodded. "You'll have to point out where the poison ivy grows."

The twins' older brother, Steven, looked up from his cereal and laughed. "They'll need help figuring out who's Elizabeth and who's Jessica, that's for sure."

"We'll have to tell them to watch out for the mean dog down the street," Elizabeth said.

"And we can take them to the city lot we

helped turn into a park." Jessica smiled as she thought about all the things she could help Eric and Wesley do. She liked the idea of being an expert. "It's a good thing I'm here," she added. "Without me, Eric and Wesley would have the worst weekend in the history of the world."

"Does that mean you'll play with us?" Elizabeth asked.

Jessica nodded. "You bet!"

CHAPTER 2

Double Trouble

"Hurray!" Jessica shouted as she hopped off the bottom step of the school bus that afternoon. "It's the weekend."

"Double hurray!" Elizabeth said, jumping down after her. "It's almost time for Eric and Wesley to get here."

Steven got off the bus after Jessica and Elizabeth. "This weekend is going to be re-e-e-eal long," he complained. "How am I going to survive with so many little kids in the house?"

"Eric and Wesley aren't little kids," Elizabeth said. "They're the same age as Jess and me."

Steven grinned. "Right. Like I said, little kids."

"Don't listen to him," Jessica told Elizabeth. She stuck out her tongue at Steven.

The twins rushed into the house and found their mother reading the newspaper in the kitchen. "Hello there," Mrs. Wakefield greeted them.

"Hi, Mom. Are Eric and Wesley here yet?" Elizabeth asked.

"Not yet," Mrs. Wakefield said. "They should arrive in about half an hour."

"Half an hour," Jessica moaned. "That's forever."

Mrs. Wakefield smiled. "Why don't you go outside and play?" she suggested. "Time will go faster that way."

"OK, but call us as soon as they get here," Elizabeth said. She grabbed Jessica's hand and pulled her out the back door. "Let's go play in the fort," she said. Elizabeth had finished building a new fort the afternoon before.

The twins ran across the backyard and into the woods behind their house. The fort was in a clearing. It was square shaped with a tree at each corner. The walls were made out of pine branches, and a blanket thrown over the walls formed the roof. Inside, the ground was covered with moss, and a tree stump served as a table.

"This is the best fort ever," Elizabeth said proudly.

"It's perfect," Jessica agreed. "We did a great job."

Elizabeth giggled. "You mean *I* did a great job."

"I helped," Jessica protested.

Elizabeth shook her head.

"OK," Jessica admitted with a smile. "I didn't help much."

She crawled inside the fort. Elizabeth followed her.

"Let's play Go Fish," Elizabeth suggested. She had brought a deck of cards and a few other games out the evening before.

"I get to shuffle the cards first," Jessica called.

"Jessica!" Mrs. Wakefield shouted a half hour later. "Elizabeth!"

Elizabeth put down the card she had just picked up. "Eric and Wesley must be here," she said. "Let's go!"

Elizabeth and Jessica crawled out of the fort and ran all the way to the house. They hurried inside. Mrs. Wakefield was sitting on the living-room couch with two other grown-ups.

"Girls, I'd like you to meet Mr. and Mrs. Nelson," Mrs. Wakefield said.

"Hello," the twins said at the same time.

"Where are Eric and Wesley?" Jessica asked.

"BOO!" A boy with curly blond hair sprang out from behind a chair. He landed right in front of Elizabeth, who jumped back in surprise.

"BLAH!" Another boy with curly blond hair leaped out from behind another chair and landed in front of Jessica. Jessica jumped twice as far as Elizabeth had.

"We got them," one of the boys shouted. He held one hand above his head.

"Excellent!" the other boy yelled, as he jumped up and slapped his brother's hand.

Elizabeth and Jessica laughed. "Watch out," Elizabeth said. "We might decide to get you back."

Mr. Nelson smiled. "This is Eric," he said, tousling the hair of the slightly bigger boy. Eric smiled.

Jessica turned to the other boy. "So you're Wesley."

"That's my name," Wesley said. "Don't wear it out."

"Eric and Wesley may *look* like angels," Mrs. Nelson told Mrs. Wakefield, "but they don't always *act* like angels." Eric and Wesley grinned proudly.

Elizabeth glanced at her sister. She had a feeling it was going to be an interesting weekend.

CHAPTER 3

The Lost Bear

When Mr. and Mrs. Nelson were ready to go, Eric and Wesley hugged their parents goodbye. Then everyone went outside and waved as the Nelsons drove away.

"We can show you around now," Jessica suggested.

"OK," Eric agreed.

The twins took Wesley and Eric to see their room.

"Too pink," Eric said with a frown.

"I have my own room," Wesley bragged.

"Hey!" Jessica said suddenly. "Where's my koala?"

Jessica and Elizabeth had matching koala bears. The bears were the twins' favorite stuffed animals, and they slept with them every night. During the day, Elizabeth's bear sat on Elizabeth's pillow, and Jessica's bear sat on Jessica's pillow. But now Jessica's bear was gone.

"I don't know where it is," Elizabeth said.

Eric and Wesley looked at each other. They didn't say anything.

"We have to find it," Jessica said, sounding upset. "It was here this morning."

She started looking under the beds and in the closet. Elizabeth ran to check the bathroom and Mr. and Mrs. Wakefield's room. She even searched Steven's room. The bear was nowhere to be found.

Slowly Elizabeth and Jessica went back to their room, where Eric and Wesley were waiting for them.

"Where do you think Jessica's bear could be?" Elizabeth asked Wesley.

"I don't think," Wesley said. "I know."

"What do you mean?" Jessica asked.

"You were outside playing when we got here," Wesley said. "While your mom showed our parents around, Eric and I came up here and found your bear. It looked bored, so we decided to send it on a vacation. We hid it in our parents' car. Your bear is on its way to Los Angeles!" He and Eric started laughing, looking very pleased with themselves.

Jessica felt terrible. She looked at Elizabeth. Elizabeth stared back at Jessica. Jessica knew they were both thinking the same thing: Out-of-town guests weren't so great, after all.

"Yummy!" Steven said, rubbing his stomach. "I can't wait to eat."

"And drink," Elizabeth added. "I love Dad's famous lemonade!"

Mr. Wakefield was making fresh lemonade to drink with dinner, while Mrs. Wakefield was making a salad. Elizabeth and Jessica were helping her. Wesley, Eric, and Steven were setting the table.

Jessica was still worried about her bear. "I hope Mr. and Mrs. Nelson don't throw away my koala," she said.

"What do you mean?" Mr. Wakefield asked, sounding puzzled.

"Wesley and Eric put Jessica's koala in their parents' car," Elizabeth explained. "It's probably in Los Angeles by now."

Steven laughed.

"It's not funny!" Jessica said angrily.

Mrs. Wakefield patted Jessica on the back. "Don't worry, your koala will be back on Sunday. Just think of the adventure it'll have had."

"Unless your koala likes Los Angeles better than Sweet Valley," Steven said. "Then it might decide to stay there."

"Ha, ha, ha," Jessica muttered.

"I'll share my koala with you until Sunday," Elizabeth whispered so that only Jessica could hear. That made Jessica feel a tiny bit better. She smiled at her sister.

Mr. Wakefield brought seven glasses to the table and filled each one from the pitcher. "There's no sugar in this lemonade," he said. "It's very sour. So help yourself from the sugar bowl."

Steven grabbed the sugar first. "I like tons of sugar in my lemonade," he announced, spooning three teaspoons into his glass. Then he pushed the sugar bowl toward Elizabeth.

"Do you want some?" Elizabeth asked Eric politely.

"You go first," Eric told her.

Elizabeth took a teaspoon of sugar and passed the bowl to Jessica. Jessica helped herself to one teaspoon, too. As she brought the glass to her lips, Steven took a big gulp of

his lemonade, and Elizabeth took a sip of hers.

"Bah!" Steven shouted, spitting his lemonade back into the glass.

Elizabeth spit her lemonade out, too. "Yuck! This is disgusting."

Wesley started to giggle. Eric was grinning.

Jessica set her glass down fast.

Mrs. Wakefield tasted a pinch of whatever was in the sugar bowl. "This is salt," she said.

"We got them!" Eric cried. He jumped up and slapped Wesley's hand.

Mr. Wakefield shook his head, smiling. "That's the oldest trick in the book."

"We all still fell for it," Steven pointed out.

Eric, Wesley, Mr. Wakefield, Mrs. Wakefield, and Steven all laughed.

"I don't think that was very funny," Elizabeth said. She sounded grumpy.

Jessica felt grumpy, too. Two days with Eric and Wesley were going to be two days too many.

CHAPTER 4

More Tricks

The next morning, Elizabeth and Jessica went into the bathroom to brush their teeth.

Elizabeth closed the door behind them. "I want to keep our guests out," she said.

"Good thinking," Jessica told her.

"Jessica," Elizabeth said a second later, "don't get upset, but there's a beetle on the soap. A huge one!"

Jessica's eyes grew wide. "Gross," she said with a gasp.

"Don't worry," Elizabeth said. "It won't hurt you."

But Jessica wasn't looking at the beetle. She was pointing to her toothbrush. There was a large black spider on it.

Elizabeth looked around and noticed three or four more bugs crawling on the walls. She didn't know what kind they were, but they were furry and had lots of legs.

"Wait a minute," Elizabeth said. "I bet these bugs are fake. They're another one of Eric and Wesley's tricks."

Jessica laughed in relief. "Right," she agreed. "There are tons of bugs in here. They couldn't all be real." She pointed to the floor. "There's a grasshopper."

"A plastic grasshopper," Elizabeth corrected her. "You can tell it's fake. It's much too big to be real."

Jessica reached down to pick up the insect, but when she touched it, the grasshopper took a giant hop toward Elizabeth.

"Aaack! Plastic bugs don't jump," Jessica yelled. "I'm getting Mom!"

But when Jessica tried to open the bathroom door, she discovered that it was locked from the outside. The twins were trapped with the bugs!

"Mom!" Jessica screamed. "Dad!"

Elizabeth wasn't usually afraid of insects. Still, having so many in one place gave her the creeps. She watched nervously as a large centipede scampered across the floor toward the bathtub. "Help!" she called out, joining her sister by the door.

On the other side of the door, the twins heard Eric and Wesley start to laugh. "We got them," Eric's voice said. "Excellent!"

Jessica pounded on the locked door. "Let us out right now!"

"We can't hear you!" Wesley yelled. "The door is closed."

Elizabeth stood close to the door. "OK. You got us. Very funny. Now let us out."

"What did you say?" Eric shouted back. "If you want to talk to us, why don't you open the door?" Both boys started laughing again.

"Mom!" Elizabeth screamed, as loudly as she could. "Dad!"

Jessica joined in. "Help!"

Finally, Mrs. Wakefield heard them and came to see what was wrong. She unlocked the bathroom door, and Elizabeth and Jessica rushed out. Elizabeth knew she and Jessica had been locked in for only a few minutes—but it had seemed like hours.

"What happened?" Mrs. Wakefield asked.

"I don't know," Eric said, shrugging. "I think Elizabeth and Jessica were stuck."

"We were trying to open the door to let them out," Wesley added.

Elizabeth was angry. "They were *not* trying to help," she said. "They were the ones who locked us in."

"Look in the bathroom," Jessica told her mom.

Mrs. Wakefield walked into the bathroom. "Oh, my," she said when she saw all the bugs. Then she started to laugh. "Breakfast is in exactly six minutes and fourteen seconds," she said, winking at Eric and Wesley. "I want all the bugs back out in the yard before then."

"Having houseguests is terrible," Jessica complained.

30

Breakfast was over, and Mrs. Wakefield was swimming with Eric and Wesley in the Wakefields' pool. The twins had gone to their fort to get away from the boys.

"You're right," Elizabeth said. "It's like having two more brothers."

"Eric and Wesley are even worse than Steven," Jessica said.

Elizabeth nodded. "They're trickier."

Jessica's face brightened. "I have a great idea. Let's play a trick on *them*," she suggested.

Elizabeth didn't usually like playing tricks on people. Then she thought about Jessica's koala, and the salty lemonade, and the bugs in the bathroom. She decided it was time to teach Wesley and Eric a lesson. She grinned. "OK, Jess. What's your plan?"

CHAPTER 5

Splash!

Jessica and Elizabeth hurried through the woods and raced across their backyard. They had come up with the perfect trick to get back at Eric and Wesley. The boys were sitting near the pool. Jessica was happy to see that they had already changed out of their bathing suits.

"Your mom went inside," Eric told her. "She's getting ready to go out."

Jessica poked Elizabeth with her elbow. Elizabeth took a deep breath. "Do you want to play soccer?" she asked.

"Sure," Wesley said.

Eric nodded. "Sounds good."

"I've got to go inside for a second," Jessica announced. She started to walk toward the house.

"Jessica doesn't like soccer," Jessica heard Elizabeth tell Wesley and Eric.

"Playing with girls is no fun, anyway," Eric said.

"Girls belong with their dumb dolls," Wesley added.

When she heard that, Jessica felt angrier than ever. Before, she had felt a tiny bit bad about playing a trick on the boys—but not anymore.

Jessica raced upstairs to her bedroom and looked in the closet. Then she searched the drawers. Then she peeked under Elizabeth's bed. Finally, she found a package of balloons under her own bed. The twins had saved the balloons from their seventh birthday party.

Jessica went into the hall and poked her head out the window that faced the backyard. "Elizabeth," she yelled. "Dad wants you."

"Coming," Elizabeth said. "I'll be right back," she told Eric and Wesley. Then she ran into the house and up the stairs.

"I found them," Jessica said, holding up the bag of balloons.

Elizabeth smiled. "Great. Let's get to work."

Elizabeth and Jessica tiptoed into the bathroom and closed the door behind them. Jessica stretched the opening of a green balloon over the sink's faucet. Elizabeth turned the cold-water tap on.

"Careful," Elizabeth said, as the balloon quickly filled with water. "Hold it steady or it'll burst." She turned off the water.

Jessica carefully removed the balloon from the faucet. It was slippery and it weighed a lot, but she managed to tie the end in a knot. Elizabeth pulled a bucket out from under the sink, and Jessica placed the balloon into it. They made enough water balloons to fill the bucket to the top.

Then the twins tiptoed into the hall, carrying the heavy bucket between them. They crouched down under the window.

"Ready?" Jessica asked.

"Ready," Elizabeth said.

Jessica stuck her head out the window. "Wesley! Eric!" she called out the window. "Come over here."

The boys looked up and saw Jessica.

Wesley tucked the soccer ball under his arm and walked toward the house, with his brother right behind him.

"What's up?" Eric asked.

When both boys were standing right below the window, Jessica glanced at her sister and nodded. "Now," she whispered.

Elizabeth jumped up. She had a water balloon in each hand. She dropped them out the window. One balloon landed on Eric's head. The other balloon exploded on the grass and got both boys wet.

"Hey!" Eric shouted.

"Cut it out!" Wesley yelled.

Elizabeth and Jessica bent to grab more balloons. When they stood up, Eric and Wesley were running away.

Jessica threw one. *Splat!* The balloon hit the ground and soaked Eric's shoes.

Elizabeth threw hers. *Splash!* She hit Wesley on the back.

"We got them!" Elizabeth yelled.

Jessica burst out laughing. Eric and Wesley were soaking wet. Their hair was plastered down on their faces. She and Elizabeth had gotten back at the boys fair and square.

CHAPTER 6

Crash!

When the twins finally ran out of water balloons, they leaned out the window.

"Hey, I thought you were finished swimming," Jessica called out to Wesley and Eric.

"Is it raining out? Why don't you use an umbrella?" Elizabeth added, laughing.

Eric and Wesley weren't laughing, though. "What did you do that for?" Eric demanded.

"You deserved it," Elizabeth said.

"Did not!" Wesley yelled.

"You did *so* deserve it," Jessica said. "For

being the worst guests in the history of the world."

"You're the worst hosts in the history of the world," Eric shot back.

"That's enough." It was Mr. Wakefield. He was standing behind Elizabeth and Jessica.

"Hello, Mr. Wakefield," Wesley called up to the twins' father. Eric smiled sweetly.

Elizabeth frowned. Eric and Wesley were too good at pretending they hadn't done anything wrong.

"Why don't you come inside and change your clothes?" Mr. Wakefield called down to the boys. Then he shut the window and turned to Elizabeth and Jessica. He didn't look angry, just serious.

"Sorry, Dad," Elizabeth whispered.

"We had to get them back," Jessica explained.

Mr. Wakefield frowned. "Eric and Wesley are your guests. I expect you to be nice to them. Attacking them with water balloons is not nice."

Elizabeth didn't understand why she and Jessica were the ones getting in trouble, when Eric and Wesley had been causing trouble ever since they arrived. "But Dad—" she began.

"No excuses," Mr. Wakefield said. "I expect you to be good hosts, even if it's hard." Mr. Wakefield walked back downstairs.

Jessica crossed her arms. "That's not fair. Eric and Wesley are allowed to play tricks on us and we can't get them back."

Elizabeth shook her head. She didn't think the boys should get special treatment, either. But there didn't seem to be anything they could do about it.

* * *

During lunch, Mr. and Mrs. Wakefield, Steven, Eric, and Wesley told knock-knock jokes. Jessica and Elizabeth weren't in the mood for any more jokes, though.

Wesley and Eric finished eating and ran out of the kitchen.

Elizabeth stood up. "Come on, Jess. Let's go play."

Mr. Wakefield smiled at Elizabeth. "Don't forget to include the boys," he said.

Jessica frowned. "Oh, all right."

Elizabeth and Jessica found Eric and Wesley in the living room. They were looking at a sports magazine.

"They're breaking the rule," Jessica whispered to Elizabeth.

Mrs. Wakefield was studying interior design and had recently redecorated the room.

It looked much prettier now. But the Wakefields had a new rule: no playing in the living room.

"I'm telling," Jessica said quietly.

Elizabeth poked Jessica in the side. "Dad said to be nice," she whispered back.

Jessica frowned. "But—"

"They're just reading a magazine," Elizabeth said. "It's OK. That's not really playing."

Jessica sighed. She and Elizabeth sat down next to the boys.

Jessica pointed to a picture of a gymnast in the magazine. "That's neat."

"I can do lots of gymnastics," Wesley boasted.

"Me, too," Eric said.

Wesley jumped up off the couch. He turned three somersaults on the rug. "Pretty good, huh?"

"That's nothing," Eric said. He jumped off the couch, turned three somersaults, then a fourth, then a fifth. He didn't stop until he bumped into the wall. The bookcase jiggled.

"Be careful," Elizabeth said.

"I bet you can't do this," Wesley said to Eric. Wesley moved over near the bookcase and put his head and hands down on the floor. He brought his legs up along the wall. Then he moved them away. Wesley held the headstand for a few seconds before letting himself down.

"I can do it for twice as long as that," Eric said. He put his head and hands down on the floor and pushed himself into a headstand. Eric held the headstand until his face turned red.

"Show off," Jessica said. "You better get down."

It was too late. Eric's arms started to shake. He tumbled to one side and smashed into the bookcase. The vase on top of the bookcase wobbled, fell over, and rolled off the shelf. Wesley tried to catch it, but he wasn't fast enough. The vase hit the floor and shattered.

Eric sat up. "What did I break?" He sounded worried.

"Mom's new vase," Jessica told him.

"Can we fix it?" Wesley asked.

"No way," Elizabeth told him. "It's in a million pieces."

Mrs. Wakefield came into the living room. "What's going on in here? Is everyone OK?"

Elizabeth, Jessica, Eric, and Wesley nodded.

"Did something break?" Mrs. Wakefield asked. She looked at the floor and saw the pieces of the broken vase. "What were you kids doing in here?" she asked sternly.

Jessica and Elizabeth exchanged glances. Elizabeth was sorry that her mother's vase had broken. But she was also secretly a little bit glad. Eric and Wesley were finally going to get what they deserved: Big Trouble.

CHAPTER 7

No Fair!

Eric took a deep breath. "It's all my fault," he told Mrs. Wakefield.

"And mine," Wesley said.

"We were doing headstands," Eric explained. "I lost my balance and fell."

"We're sorry," Wesley said.

"It's OK," Mrs. Wakefield told the boys. "Accidents happen. But please don't play in here again. No playing in the living room is an important rule in this house."

"They're not in trouble?" Elizabeth asked.

"No, they're not in trouble," Mrs. Wakefield said. "They didn't know the living-room rule. But you girls *did* know it. You should have told Eric and Wesley not to play in here. I'm disappointed in you two."

Jessica felt her eyes fill with tears. Eric and Wesley had been causing trouble since they arrived. But she and Elizabeth were always getting blamed for everything. It wasn't fair!

The telephone rang. "I'd better get that," Mrs. Wakefield said. "Why don't you play upstairs? I'll clean up the mess in here later."

Jessica gave Eric and Wesley an angry look and stomped out of the living room. Elizabeth stomped out after her.

"We didn't do anything wrong," Jessica said, when they got to their bedroom.

Elizabeth sat down on her bed. "I wish Eric and Wesley had never come," she said.

"I wish they'd never been born," Jessica added.

Wesley and Eric appeared in the twins' doorway.

Wesley grinned. "Wait till you see what we're going to do next."

Eric pulled on Wesley's arm. "Come on. Let's get started." The boys ran out of the room and down the stairs.

Jessica groaned. "What do you think they're up to?"

"Something awful," Elizabeth said. "I wish we could run away and not come home until they're gone."

Jessica's face lit up. "That's a great idea! Why don't we run away? No one will miss us."

"I guess not," Elizabeth agreed. "But where would we go?"

Jessica thought for a minute. "How about Grandma's?"

"No way," Elizabeth said. "Grandma and Grandpa would send us home."

"Oh, yeah. You're right." Jessica closed her eyes and tried to think of someplace else.

"I've got it," Elizabeth said suddenly.

Jessica opened her eyes.

Elizabeth was smiling. "The fort."

CHAPTER 8

The Runaways

"Do we need anything else?" Elizabeth asked.

Jessica studied the pile of stuff on Elizabeth's bed. There were two peanut-butter-and-jelly sandwiches, two apples, and six chocolate-chip cookies. There were also two matching sweatshirts, Elizabeth's three favorite toy cars, and Jessica's pink-satin change purse with a dime inside.

"I think we have everything important," Jessica said. "I'd bring my koala if I still had it," she added with a frown.

Thinking about Jessica's koala made Elizabeth angry all over again. "Running away is the best idea we ever had," she said. She took her own koala from her pillow and added it to the pile.

Jessica and Elizabeth put the sandwiches, apples, cookies, sweatshirts, cars, purse, and koala into Jessica's pink backpack. Jessica picked it up, and the twins sneaked down the stairs and into the kitchen. Nobody was in sight.

"Wait," Elizabeth said, as her sister was about to open the back door.

"What is it?" Jessica whispered.

"We forgot something important," Elizabeth whispered back. "When you run away, you're supposed to leave a note."

"That's right," Jessica agreed. "We've got to leave a note."

Elizabeth found a pen and a piece of paper,

and quickly wrote a note. She read it over, then put it under a magnet on the refrigerator.

"You have been mean and we're very, very mad," the note said. *"We're going far away. We might come back someday. But not until you-know-who go home. Love, Liz and Jess."*

Then Elizabeth and Jessica left the house and crossed the backyard. When they reached the edge of the woods, Elizabeth stopped and turned around.

"Why are you stopping?" Jessica asked.

"I want to take one last look at our house," Elizabeth told her.

Jessica turned around, too. She felt like crying. She wished they didn't have to run away. But they had no choice as long as Eric and Wesley were there.

Elizabeth took Jessica's hand and led the way to the fort. When they got there, they crawled inside and sat down on the moss floor. It wasn't dinnertime yet, but running away made the twins hungry. They unwrapped their sandwiches and started to eat.

"This is the best fort in the whole world," Jessica said suddenly. "Do you know why?"

Elizabeth shook her head. "Why?"

"No boys!" Jessica said.

"No boys!" Elizabeth agreed with a laugh. She still felt a little bit sad, though. "Do you think Mom and Dad will miss us?"

"I hope so," Jessica said. "Then they'll be sorry they were so mean!"

CHAPTER 9

Strange Noises

It was almost dinnertime, and past the time Elizabeth and Jessica were usually safe at home.

Screech! Scratch!

Elizabeth and Jessica were not safe at home. They were still sitting in the fort. It was pitch-black outside. It was also pitch-black inside, because the twins had forgotten to bring a flashlight.

Scratch! Screech!

"Are you afraid?" Jessica asked as she listened to the strange noises coming from outside.

"No," Elizabeth said slowly. "There's nothing to be afraid of."

Jessica relaxed. Having a brave sister was nice. She moved closer to Elizabeth, and her hand brushed against Elizabeth's knee. Elizabeth jumped.

"What was that?" Elizabeth asked anxiously.

Jessica giggled. "It was just my hand."

Elizabeth let out a sigh of relief.

"I'm hungry," Jessica complained. The chocolate-chip cookies and the apples were gone. All that was left was half of a peanut-butter-and-jelly sandwich, and it was completely squashed. "I wonder what's for dinner tonight?" she added.

"I wouldn't care if it was brussels sprouts and beef stew," Elizabeth said.

Jessica wrinkled her nose. Brussels

sprouts and beef stew were two of the foods the twins liked least. But Jessica knew what Elizabeth meant. It would be wonderful to be home for dinner, no matter what they had to eat.

"I miss Mom and Dad," Jessica said.

Elizabeth hugged her sister. "I know. I even miss Steven."

"Me, too," Jessica said. "But I guess they don't miss us. If they did, they would have come looking for us and we wouldn't be here anymore."

Suddenly the twins heard voices. "Jessica! Elizabeth!" one voice called out. It was Mrs. Wakefield.

"Liz! Jess!" the twins heard next. It was Mr. Wakefield.

Jessica and Elizabeth heard Steven, Eric, and Wesley shouting their names, too.

"Do you think we should go out?" Elizabeth asked.

Jessica bit her lip. "Not yet," she said. "I'm still mad."

"OK, we'll stay," Elizabeth agreed.

They listened to Mr. and Mrs. Wakefield, Steven, Eric, and Wesley calling them. The voices got nearer. Then they faded away.

"What was that?" Jessica asked. She sounded scared.

"What was what?" Elizabeth asked.

"I heard something," Jessica whispered. "Listen!"

Jessica squeezed Elizabeth's hand. Neither one of them said a word.

Crunch!

Elizabeth and Jessica jumped. The noise was coming from just outside their fort. It sounded like an animal moving through the woods.

64

Crunch!

Jessica and Elizabeth hugged each other.

Crunch! Crunch!

Jessica was afraid to breathe. She hugged Elizabeth tighter.

Then she gasped when a head poked into the fort. It was Eric. He shone a flashlight into the twins' eyes. "Wow!" he said. "What a cool fort!"

Elizabeth and Jessica exchanged relieved glances. For once, they were glad to see him.

Wesley was right behind his brother. "This is great!" he said.

Jessica could tell the boys weren't teasing. They really liked the fort.

Mr. and Mrs. Wakefield and Steven poked their heads in next. "Wow is right," Mr. Wakefield said. "This is better than any fort I ever had."

Elizabeth smiled. "Thanks," she said.

"We just found your note," Mrs. Wakefield told the twins.

"We were worried," Eric said. He sounded as if he meant it.

Wesley nodded. "We're sorry we played so many tricks on you."

"I'm sorry, too," Mrs. Wakefield said. "I could have told the boys about the living-room rule myself."

"We're all sorry," Mr. Wakefield added. "I didn't give you girls a chance to explain about the water balloons."

"*I'm* not apologizing," Steven said. "I didn't do anything wrong."

Everyone laughed.

Jessica felt much happier. "It's OK. I guess I'm not mad anymore."

Elizabeth was smiling. "Me, neither."

The twins scrambled out of the fort. Mr. and Mrs. Wakefield gave them each a big hug. "You two had me worried," Mrs. Wakefield said. "Next time you're unhappy about something, let's talk about it, OK?"

"OK," the twins agreed.

Jessica took Mr. Wakefield's hand. "Were you worried too, Dad?"

Mr. Wakefield grinned. "Not at first. I thought you'd come home when you got hungry. But I guess you were holding out pretty well."

"That's what you think," Jessica said. "What's for dinner?"

"Spaghetti with meatballs," Steven told Jessica. "Now that we found you, we can finally eat. I'm starved."

Jessica and Elizabeth exchanged smiles. Spaghetti with meatballs was one of their favorite dishes.

"I'm glad we're not running away any-more," Elizabeth said.

"Me, too," Jessica agreed. "The fort is great, but home is the nicest place on earth. Especially at dinnertime."

CHAPTER 10

Friends at Last

"Can we play in the fort?" Wesley asked the twins after breakfast the next morning. "Please?"

"Sure," Elizabeth said. "We can make believe we're Indians."

"The fort will be our tepee," Jessica added.

"Let's go!" Eric said.

Elizabeth, Jessica, Eric, and Wesley raced to the fort. When they got there, Eric pretended to be Old Chief Buffalo Breath. He sat in the tepee all morning and gave orders. Elizabeth and Wesley were braves. They practiced walking through the woods without making a sound. Jessica was the medicine woman. She gathered leaves and berries to make a pretend healing potion.

"Boys! Girls!" they heard a woman shout.

"That's our mom," Wesley said.

Eric and Wesley ran through the woods. Elizabeth and Jessica followed them. The boys didn't stop running until they reached their parents. Mr. and Mrs. Nelson gave each of the boys a big hug.

"Hurray!" Wesley shouted, dancing in a circle around Mr. and Mrs. Nelson. "Mom and Dad are back!"

A few minutes later, Eric and Wesley were ready to go. The Wakefields watched as the boys put their bags into the Nelsons' car. Mr. and Mrs. Wakefield, Steven, Elizabeth, and Jessica waved as the Nelsons started to drive away. But before it reached the end of the street, the Nelsons' car jerked to a stop and Wesley jumped out. He ran back to the Wakefields.

"I almost forgot," he said when he reached them. He held out Jessica's koala bear.

"I did forget," Jessica told Wesley, taking the bear from him and giving it a big hug. "Thanks."

"You're welcome," Wesley said. He turned and ran back to the car.

"Too bad Eric and Wesley live so far away," Jessica said as the Nelsons' station wagon disappeared around the corner.

Elizabeth giggled. "Does that mean you didn't mind being invaded?"

Jessica laughed. "Nope. It was fun."

"Things are going to be boring without Eric and Wesley," Elizabeth said.

"No, they won't," Jessica reminded her. "A new boy is starting school next week. Remember?"

The Friday before, their teacher, Mrs. Otis, had announced that a new student was joining their second-grade class.

"That's right," Elizabeth said.

"What's the new boy's name again?" Jessica asked. "Mrs. Otis wrote it on the board."

"I don't remember," Elizabeth said. "But I copied it down."

"Let's go look," Jessica suggested.

They ran into the house and upstairs to their room. Jessica put her koala back on her pillow where it belonged. Elizabeth found the new boy's name written on a piece of paper. "Kisho Murasaki," Elizabeth read.

"Kisho Murasaki," Jessica repeated. "That's a cool name."

Elizabeth nodded. "Kisho and I are going to be friends."

Jessica laughed. "Wait until you meet him," she said. "He might be a bigger troublemaker than Eric and Wesley."

"No way!" Elizabeth said. "I'm sure he'll be great."

Will Kisho be as nice as Elizabeth imagines? Find out in Sweet Valley Kids #32, LEFT BACK!